# Clifford's
## Happy Easter

**Norman Bridwell**

SCHOLASTIC INC.
New York Toronto London Auckland
Sydney Mexico City New Delhi Hong Kong

For Lauren Nicole Delker



Library of Congress Cataloging-in-Publication Data is available.

ISBN 978-0-545-21587-9

12 11 10 9 8 7 6 5 4 3 2 1     11 12 13 14 15

Printed in the U.S.A. 40
This edition first printing, January 2011

Hi! I'm Emily Elizabeth, and I love spring.
So does my dog, Clifford.

The best part of springtime is Easter.

Last spring Mom and Dad brought us a lot of eggs to color for the big Easter egg hunt.

On the day before Easter, I dyed the eggs.

Clifford wanted to help.

Poor Clifford. He wasn't very good at painting eggs.

So Clifford helped by watching me decorate the eggs.
He's a good watcher.

When I went to bed that night,
I fell asleep dreaming about Easter eggs.

It was a beautiful dream. Clifford was stirring a giant tub of dye while I tossed in the eggs.

But then Clifford lost his balance!
He tumbled into the tub of dye.

Something surprising began to happen. . . .

Suddenly Clifford was bright green!

It was just like St. Patrick's Day.

Then he turned sunshine yellow!
This was becoming a very strange dream.

I grabbed a brush and began to dab on purple polka dots.

Clifford looked good in polka dots, but—

— they didn't last long.
The purple dots turned into squares,
and Clifford looked like . . .

. . . a giant checkerboard!

I didn't like that. I threw on some more dye.

Clifford started to change colors again.

Now he was red, white, and blue!

I always used to wonder if I dreamed in color.

Now I know.

This was too much.

I tried to scrub the dye off Clifford. I was getting frantic...

. . . then I woke up.

It was Easter morning, and the sun was shining.

I ran out to see Clifford.

Thank goodness he looked just the same as always.

Good old Clifford.

We joined my friends and set off on the Easter egg hunt.

We looked high.

We looked low.

Clifford looked in places I would not have thought of.

No hiding place was missed.

Sometimes Clifford went a little too far.

His hard work helped.

We ended up with heaps of eggs . . .

. . . which we shared with our friends.

After all, friends are what make Easter a happy day.